Nameless

Nameless

Dawn M. Keiser

SANTA ROSA, CA

Published by
Athena Star Press
2467 Westvale Court, Santa Rosa, California, 95403, USA
http://athenastarpress.com

In association with
Under the Red Fedora
http://www.undertheredfedora.com

ISBN: 978-1-60038-072-3 (Paperback)
ISBN: 978-1-60038-073-0 (Hardcover)
ISBN: 978-1-60038-074-7 (Kindle)

Cover art by Emily Robinson
Cover design by Dawn M. Keiser
Edited by Marina Michaels

Library of Congress Control Number: 2020943303

Originally published in the United States with the
Silver Ink Writers group in the 2018 anthology of short stories *Silver Linings*,
and edited by Kait Prader.

*This book is dedicated to
my best friend, confidant, and father Steven,
my late stepmother Carole,
and all those who taught me
it's okay to keep it weird.*

Acknowledgements

The sheer number of people who have helped me bring this story to life is too vast and varied to capture in such a short space, but I would like to thank a few in particular for their pivotal contributions:

My tabletop gaming group – particularly Jordon, Chris, Marina, Liz, and Andrew – for inspiring me and enthusiastically allowing me to use our game sessions as a place to explore my characters.

Georgette and the rest of the Snoopy's Writers, a wondrous and thoughtful group who are always as equally prepared to discuss the state of the world as they are to share a few whimsies, a new story, or some poetry.

My friend, cheerleader, and first editor Kait, and my friend James, for helping make the Silver Ink Writers group possible, which led to the first ever publication of this story.

My editor, friend, and all-around amazing woman Marina, who not only helped inspire one of the pivotal characters of Otherland, has listened patiently to endless hours of my ramblings on how this fictional world has expanded and evolved over the years, (and agreed to be my editor despite my rather unapologetic irreverence to the notion of 'proper English').

My dear friend Emily for her fantastic artwork, and for being one of those incredible people who can pick up a conversation where we left off, even if it's been a year (or three).

And all those who helped me along the way, whether it was dealing with my endless requests for opinions and input, or providing general support to help me get through each day.

Thank you! I couldn't have done this without all of you in my life.

The Fortune Teller

THE first time she meets him, he is already quite familiar with the Tea Shop. Despite not feeling his presence until heavy, dirt encrusted boots step across the threshold of the front door, she can hear the joy in the Tea Shop's chimes, a subtle welcome for the strange figure.

The others stir beneath the surface of her Fortune Teller form as he enters, but in confusion, not recognition. She has not yet changed from her last visitor, and for the briefest moment her hand trembles over a cup of steaming tea. Surprise is an unfamiliar experience, and most assuredly unwelcome. She finally lets her eyes rest on the man in old jeans and an older jacket, and knows he is not one of the Tea

Shop's potentials, nor was he ever meant to be. His apparent and clear disconnect from her world of heroes' journeys and grandiose destinies – or more specifically, her role in that world – piques an interest not tied to any form. The Fortune Teller fades around the edges, the Seer and the Harbinger battling for prominence. She holds them all in check, while the others watch behind her eyes in barely restrained curiosity.

She hides the teacup and tray, and turns half-closed eyes towards the stranger entering her space. He is shuffling into the Tea Shop with a hesitance that belies his familiarity with the place. The man knows where he is, but is not quite certain of his welcome.

"I know I was rude," his voice is gruff, and yet... she faces him and opens up her senses to fully look.

"Apparently so." She knows her voice is quiet, uncommitted, and yet cannot make an effort to ease the growing tension in his frame. This is too rare an occurrence.

They are out of sync, and while such switchbacks in storylines were to be expected in her existence, she always knew ahead of time. She was always prepared. This disruption...she is not certain what to be more shocked over: that the Tea Shop had allowed it or that it has happened at all.

How intriguing.

The man before her looks haggard, weary over some internal battle that wages behind his eyes, yet he meets her gaze straight on.

He opens his mouth, then shuts it again, before taking an unsteady breath. "I'm sorry."

"I know." And she does, though she knows it is for some other version of her to grant him the absolution he is after. So she takes from his mind only what she needs to send him on his way with enough courage to return. "Coffee?"

"Please." He makes no other comment, though a question flickers in the back of his mind before being pushed down, perhaps in the interest of appeasing her.

Her long, layered dress swirls as dramatically as her wild, frizzy hair when she comes sweeping around the counter – a drama that had been necessary for getting through to her last visitor – and places two hot mugs of coffee onto the table closest to him.

They sit across from each other in silence, him drinking his coffee in slow, awkward sips, as she pretends to taste the smooth dark brew while using those moments to study him. Perhaps it is remnants of the Fortune Teller, or the barely restrained presence of the Harbinger under her skin, but she realizes rather abruptly that this stranger could become as familiar a feature in the Tea Shop as the bell above the front door and the unpredictable mood of the back door.

"Can I come back?" he asks. His words interrupt the thread of panic growing at the potential future she has begun to see.

She returns her focus to him, and gives a nod, just barely resisting the urge to reach into his mind for more. A curiosity she has never known burns within her, and she scratches at her fingertips to ease the sensation. He notices, and yet once again makes no remark.

Interesting.

"Am I forgiven?"

A hitch in his tone gives her pause. She narrows her eyes and barely brushes the surface of his mind. His question is sincere, but he is also prodding for an answer to a question that has not fully formed in his conscious mind. He knows, somehow, that something is fundamentally different between them.

Even more interesting.

She pulls back into herself once more and sets her mug down between them.

"That isn't something I can give you."

He looks like he might plead his case, though he holds back whatever words he was summoning when she raises her hand.

"That isn't something I can give you yet."

Realization deflates him.

"You don't know me, do you?"

She shakes her head, and the part of her that would come to know him aches a bit at his expression. On some unfamiliar instinct she reaches for him, then thinks better of it. He seems both too fragile and too hardened, a brittle glass soul sitting on a ledge.

He stands abruptly. "I should go."

Too soon. Left in this state he may not come back, and a for a moment the Seer pushes through just enough to show her an image of fire and rage, oily flames crawling through the Tea Shop while inky darkness seeps from her fingers and chokes out each spark of life within reach.

She stands, hair and skirts swirling, obsidian skin shimmering in the light from the windows, and grips his arm. Silence strains between them until he reluctantly meets her gaze.

"I do not know you yet," she whispers and pushes the words to him with as much power as she dares. "That does not mean she is gone. She's still here." *Come back, Duke. Come back to us.*

He reaches up and hesitantly brushes a thumb over her cheek. Her skin is warm. His face is unreadable.

As the door clicks closed behind him, the flames in her mind fade to a muted, unknown swirl. She presses her palms to her cheeks. The future may still yet be undecided, but at least one fate has been averted.

For now.

The Beginnings of Self

SHE is more prepared for him the next time.

"I guess that answers that question," he says without context or humor. She feels the echo of a question he asked long ago, one that she will face sometime in her nebulous future.

Do you live time in order?

She gives him the closest thing to a smile her current form can muster.

"May I?" he asks, gesturing to a dark, cozy corner of the Tea Shop that now cradles two upholstered chairs and a worn, sturdy table marked with burns and scrapes from both their pasts.

She nods.

She wants to reach for him, to gather his truths close and study them and yet, she still does not know how he fits into her purpose. So she scrutinizes him with her form's eyes instead.

He is older than his first visit, not so much in years she reckons, but in his carriage. His shoulders are hunched, grey peppers his temples, and he holds the mug of coffee she hands him with a tightness that contradicts the grateful nod he sends her way. The light in the Tea Shop begins to change before she finally breaks the silence.

"What do you need me to say?"

His face changes, mouth pulling tight around a sigh he buries by brushing his face with a calloused hand.

You make him sad, a voice whispers up in her mind, and she stills, trying to understand.

The mystery of his presence should not exist in her world.

"You don't know your name," he says instead of answering.

"I don't have a name."

"Not yet," he pushes. Static and darkness blur at the edge of her senses, the sensation of flames crawling up her skin.

"Stop," she whispers. "If I learn what is coming, they may destroy it before it can be born."

Duke slams the mug down on the table. He picks at a scorch mark he is already familiar with.

"They…" He looks at her with a scalding type of anger. "'They' your makers or 'they' those creatures that lurk beneath your skin?"

Her current form holds steady, but something in her cringes at the accusation.

"I don't know," she pauses, raising her hand to stop him from interrupting. "It may be that I am not ready to know, or –" she glances at the bell above the door. "Or it may be that they could learn too soon of the storm."

"That's not good enough."

Something crackles under her skin. A Change is coming, and she knows she has only moments before he must leave.

The Tea Shop darkens, and she feels a blanket of solitude wrap itself around them. She is fairly certain who is out there watching over her, over them, and she spares a thought in gratitude. Then she grabs his hand and tightens her grip until pain wrinkles the corners of his eyes.

"You know what's coming in a way I do not – cannot understand yet." She searches his eyes for understanding. "There is more than us at stake, and if this," she gestures between them before grabbing his other hand and bringing them both together between hers. "If this fails, everything will burn away."

"You don't know what you're asking of me," his voice is rough. *I can't lose you.* The truth breaks free of him for just a moment, just long enough for her to realize that through him her own end is coming.

9

She rests her head against their joined hands, and feels a piece of Self begin to coalesce, to solidify and take root deep within her forms.

The first birth that is all her own.

"I'm asking you to let our future keep its course."

He tries to pull his hands away.

"Please, Duke," she whispers. She lets him go, and his careful retreat makes her wonder if she has said the wrong thing. His deep sigh is all she needs to know that whatever is to come has not been broken. He speaks anyway.

"There's going to come a day when I tell you I can't accept whatever this is that's going on, whatever storm that's coming. But when it's all over," he coughs once, trying to mask the break in his voice. "When this is done, I'll be at the cabin with the puppies. And we'll be waiting for you."

His pain batters the emerging form of The Empath, confusing her senses and burying the brand new Self deep within her.

"Duke?"

He recognizes the beginnings of this form, and spits out a curse. For his last time, he cups her face in his hands and presses a kiss to her forehead.

"Goodbye, my Nameless One."

The bell above the front door remains silent as he leaves.

It

THE first time he meets her, Duke is long past battle weary and suspicious. A life of struggling for every moment of peace, an existence of warfare and paranoia and loss, has buried what little gentleness remains under layers of self-hatred and apathy.

She has had the odd pleasure of his presence a few times since the oldest version of him said goodbye, and each time he has had the advantage of a longer history between them. So she is surprised when she reaches her mind to him and finds it far more barricaded than it has ever been before.

Duke has found the Tea Shop for the first time.

For the average visitor, their first steps into the Tea Shop are a surprise, even if they have been searching for this place for decades. And the average visitor always comes through the front door. Duke has been looking, though not necessarily for the Tea Shop or even for her, and when he enters, it is through the back door.

How unsurprising.

The day in the world outside the Tea Shop's back door is overcast and blustery, and a sharp slap of chilled air follows him through before quickly dissipating into the Shop's cozy warmth. Sunlight streams through the frosted windows at the front of the shop, the only wall with a view to the outside – even if that view always seems to change upon opening the front door.

She stays out of sight and watches him. Outwardly, he gives away nothing. Still, she knows how long it takes for Duke's eyes to adjust, can feel his surprise, and is aware of the moment he begins to assess the Tea Shop. Decorated ceilings arch up into shadow, intricately painted and carved panels curving into obscurity behind the ambient light. The bell above the front door chimes untouched, and the sweet notes echo up the vaulted ceiling to dance among the rafters just out of sight.

He is hesitant, though his steps never falter as he walks intentionally into the heart of the Tea Shop and makes a slow turn. The Tea Shop seems small, despite its size, and the clutter of mismatched chairs and tables look homey instead of chaotic. Tall, sturdy shelves are overstuffed with books, knick-knacks, tea cups, and chocolate sets, and display an uncountable number of jars containing tea, coffee, and spices. Far into a hidden corner, mostly obscured by more bookshelves, is a large, thickly upholstered arm chair in front of a grand fireplace with a flagstone hearth.

When Duke has finished his turn, she steps from shadows of the Tea Shop's making, into view behind the cluttered counter directly across from the front door. A display case of tea cakes, scones, and small sandwiches shines temptingly on the counter between them. He does not even glance at them, and the only evidence that he is startled by her sudden appearance is that his scowl deepens almost imperceptibly.

She gives him a moment to study her, just as she has been studying him. Behind the walls of this hollowed out, raw version of the man, she senses a tiny spark, the barest hope of a chance at something better. It is buried too deep for her forms to touch or influence, but she already knows that something in him is willing to hold on fast to that light.

He looks at her with a hard expression, and she knows exactly what he sees: a matronly woman of indeterminate age, dark skin and wide eyes, with faint laugh lines around her mouth. The Wise Woman's dark, dusty brown hair hangs in a messy braid over one shoulder, and she wears a loose green and brown fairy dress with gold stitched into the hems.

Non-threat.

Easily manipulated.

Prey.

He means them harm.

Deep within her there is being without name or conscience, a feral intelligence at the heart of all her forms, yet unhindered by their identities. The threat he considers beckons It, and It rises behind her eyes to simmer just beneath the surface. He sees, or perhaps just senses, the shift in her, and It feels approval at the unconscious falter in his step, the instinctual recognition of a monster in another form. He reaches for his knife without fully knowing why.

When he opens his mouth to speak, she can taste the lies he is about to spin. It is indignant that he would try, even now, to gain the upper hand.

"Be careful, Duke." It gleefully lets the darkness bleed through her words and echo in his understanding. He is afraid now, even if he doesn't comprehend why, and It smirks while wearing the Wise Woman's face. The once gold thread of her garments gleam a sharp silver, the soft browns hardening into black as she crosses the cozy Tea Shop in a glide that has him retreating to the front door. The bell chimes, amused, and the sound sets both of them on edge.

Her brown hair coils in its braid, shining a metallic blood red. She stands in front of him, arms crossed, and It, still wearing the Wise Woman's face, furrows her brow as his fear transforms into awe in a matter of seconds.

"I can taste your lies, Duke," she draws out his name. "And I can see the truth of everyone who walks into my domain." He does not know that he is the only exception, that she cannot see all his truths. Because he was never meant to meet her.

His emotions are a panicked mess of fear and wonder, the internal battle causing his hands to clench reflexively. A part of him considers violence.

"Don't worry," she gives him a sly grin. "You're not meant to die here today. Your intentions, however, are bleeding through your edges as we speak." She grabs his wrists and holds them easily in place, then leans in close to whisper in his ear. "The Tea Shop would never have let you enter if you were a real threat." He shudders.

Were it not for their future, and a memory of the Tea Shop engulfed in oily flames, she would lose the struggle to rein It in before It consumed him where he stood. Instead, after a tense moment, the Wise Woman settles back into her skin and gives him a motherly smile.

She drifts over to the counter, appearing as unconcerned at turning her back to him as she is about the espresso she begins to prepare. He finds it disconcerting and she allows herself to enjoy his discomfort. No longer certain why he has come here in the first place, his steps are hesitant before he finally sits on the sturdiest looking chair in the room.

"Cozy place you got here," he says lamely, and the Wise Woman laughs. It is the laugh of every wise woman, all soft bells and singing stars and knowing. He wonders if it is a laugh that is fully hers or just for show, and his thoughts are just strong enough for her to hear.

"So what has brought Duke Hartmore, fixer for hire, to the Tea Shop?" She asks as she places the steaming mug in front of him, made just the way he likes it only better. He is not surprised to find that she already knows his name, but he is shocked at the lack of judgment she seems to have for him.

"What's your name?" He asks instead.

"I run the Tea Shop." She sits gracefully in front of him, all presence of the darkness hidden. Or gone. He can't really tell.

"That's not a name."

"It is... as close as you are going to get," she raises her eyebrows and gives him a pointed look. "Considering you came in here with violent intentions."

He has the good grace to look ashamed. "I wouldn't have killed you," he protests.

She looks at him, and he knows she can see his truths. He genuinely has no idea where he has found himself.

"No," she murmurs. "I don't suppose you would have."

"Does that mean you'll tell me your name?" He grins, and the sudden change in demeanor transforms him. More of his truths begin to bubble to the surface. It reminds her of clouds of sea foam, frothing around rocks and over sand castles.

"No," she smiles. "But I may tell you where you are, since you apparently have no idea which world you have stumbled into."

His chagrin is not faked. "It's been one hell of a day."

She nods in understanding.

"My question for you is," the Wise Woman pauses for effect, and it makes him raise his gaze to meet her eyes despite himself. "Once you know where you are heading, are you going to want to return to where you were?"

There is so much more to her question, and he knows it, can almost sense the presence of the Harbinger, and the Lover, and the Godmother, and even It underneath the Wise Woman, within the depths of her words. But it is not their presence in her that he responds to, it is the seemingly real curiosity she has at his answer.

"I don't know," he answers honestly and drains the mug in his typical manner-less fashion before setting it carefully back on the little coaster. "But if you keep brewing this glorious stuff, I know I'll be coming back here." His words are a truth, told plainly and without pretense or motive. The promise behind them makes her smile, and the hope that it is a smile all her own makes him grin.

He returns within a week.

The Gunslinger

SHE stands guard in front of the Tea House, unwilling to let her task stain the inside of her sanctuary. Men she has been waiting for yet never met have arrived on a violent search for leverage against an oppressor. The Gunslinger is here to make sure they fail – if only to ensure that the son of one of them can succeed where they will not. Assuming, of course, that child chooses justice over revenge. A choice that will come later, and that she will influence with another version of her.

They know the Gunslinger is the enforcer of their hated overlord, and they have come to make sure he cannot enforce any more injustices. They do not see the Tea Shop behind her, and do not realize that to the Gunslinger, they are merely pawns in another's story.

She is taking her first life of the day when she senses his gaze, and realizes that Duke's path has become inextricably twined with hers, despite his lack of place in this world. He is on a rooftop, looking at her through the scope of a modified re-curve, and his thoughts are so strong she can feel them as if he were shouting them aloud.

His mission had been simple: find the Gunslinger and take him out of the equation so that some evil boss would be left without their bodyguard. For once a job helping the right side. Also, no questions asked and payment up front, just as he preferred for his under-the-table work. Of course, no questions didn't mean no recon. His usual channels all confirmed one thing: the Gunslinger was competent, dangerous, and a complete mystery. And wherever the Gunslinger went, death often followed close behind.

Three months, two almost completely disparate worlds, and at least half a dozen uncomfortable alliances burned past the point of redemption later, and Duke had a sneaking suspicion that this job was over even his head. Then an anonymous tip had him up on this roof looking over the storefront of a disturbingly familiar Tea Shop, and a Gunslinger with familiar eyes.

You have got *to be kidding me.*

Duke knows that the figure below has to be the lady of the Tea Shop, even if her current form looks more like a wolf

– sleek and feral – than any of those he has met in his past few visits. He has no doubt that nothing he could shoot at her would come anywhere close to finding its mark. Even if he wanted it to.

He packs away his bow, and sprints along the rooftops to get closer. The perfect vantage point on top of the Tea Shop appears before him without effort. Watching her take the life of the poor men below, Duke suddenly finds himself unsure whose side he should be on. As if summoned by his thoughts, something collapses under his weight.

Duke expects pain, sharp edges and blunt walls, but he is tumbling rather gently down, and down, and down. He loses count at three stories, yet keeps falling. The rafters and walls are covered in broken shards of tea china, and torn paintings of crying faces.

Her faces.

He tumbles through the back door of the Tea Shop, knocking over a chair and smacking his head against a perfectly placed table.

Yup, he thinks before passing out, *the Tea Shop is grumpy with me.*

When he comes to, she is standing over him, blood drying and tacky on her hands, twirling one of his knives with a beautiful and complex precision he can only dream of one day accomplishing. The feral darkness of It simmers underneath the Gunslinger, pushing to be let loose on the man who should not be there. Out of all her forms, only It sees Duke as an affront to their existence.

He gives her his best little boy grin and hopeful expression.

"You should not exist here," It hisses. The knife continues its hypnotic dance. Duke splays his hands in surrender.

"Sorry?" *I would never turn on you.*

She says nothing. The Gunslinger has no need of the raw tamelessness It prefers to exude, she has perfected using It's darkness as a pointed weapon. She unleashes its keen edge and presses the tip of the blade to his neck. Her eyes are black. For a moment, she recognizes herself in him.

He is wondering if this is his moment, and there is... relief in that thought. She yanks herself away from him, his truth burning through the rage of her forms, and the bells above the door chime quietly, breaking the tense silence.

She laughs, harsh and barking. His grin feels frozen on his face, and he cannot help the flinch when she tosses the knife aside. Duke chooses not to stand until the Gunslinger has put a bit of space between them.

The newest Self, not yet strong enough to take shape, attempts to pull the darker forms back underneath. Most of her selves hate the monsters amongst them, and with their help, she buries the harmful fury into the deepest parts of her. The Gunslinger becomes brittle as the violence that gives her purpose is temporarily muffled. Cracks form along her skin where dried blood has begun to flake off, and her grip on one of the tables leaves behind finger-sized gouge marks.

Duke watches in horrified fascination.

"You should leave," she manages to growl out.

"What's happening?" Panic makes his voice shake a bit.

"The Gunslinger has more work to do." Inky black tears burn from her eyes, and the newest Self chokes with the pain of it.

He swallows, and tries not to vomit. "Are you trying to stop the Gunslinger?"

She nods, eyes squeezing shut.

"Have you ever tried to say no before?" He regrets the question even as he utters it. She curls in, one arm wrapping around her stomach as if his words physically hurt.

Another crack forms, smaller threads spidering out along her skin.

The sky darkens, snuffing the light that had come from the windows of the Tea Shop. Suddenly there is the sound of waves crashing against walls and echoing off the rafters.

"Not in many generations," the voice is not from either of them. A wild, red-haired woman with dark skin and stormy eyes stands in the center of the Tea Shop, abruptly blocking Duke's view of the failing Gunslinger. The woman is striking, with a long shining coat that does little to hide the sword on her hip or sea salt on her boots.

"Valentine?" The Self and other forms tremble, the Gunslinger bares her teeth, and It snarls.

"I am here." Valentine sighs and places a hand on the other woman's shoulder. Where the Gunslinger stood, a child collapses to the floor, unconscious. Spiderweb-like cracks still mark her arms and neck, but the smaller ones already show signs of fading. "My foolish comrade."

Valentine turns her gaze to Duke, and the eyes that now stare at him are not the same as when the woman had first appeared.

"You were never meant to be her target," the voice has changed as well, holding within it secrets he is certain only gods could comprehend. "Nor were you to have any part in this story. And yet... she risked her existence to keep you from harm." She looks between Duke and the sleeping child, and hums a bit.

"What do you mean, risked her existence?"

She circles him, poking at his garments, his hair, and the already healing nick on his neck where the Gunslinger had pressed his own blade to his flesh. He barely keeps himself from recoiling.

"Curiouser and curiouser," she murmurs. When she is done, she stands next to him, watching the sleeping child.

"She is not a person," Valentine's voice has changed again, at once soft and windswept, while maintaining an echo of a more powerful other. "Not in the way you are, at least. She is a vessel."

"For what?"

"Personas, tasks, catalysts," her shoulders have drooped, mouth pulling tight against some mixture of frustration and sadness. "Her purpose is to be whatever is needed to maintain the balance of the stories of the people who live in this world."

"Seriously?"

"Yes," Valentine turns to him. "If she fights directly against the reason for her existence, she risks being... remade. It is a fail-safe her creators put in place to keep her from disrupting the balance."

"That's barbaric," Duke stares at the child on the floor, skin now unblemished and smooth, and begins to understand how deep those fractures had really gone. Valentine's hand against his chest startles his attention back to the woman, and there are swirling, dark galaxies within her eyes.

"I'm sorry, Duke," she whispers in a voice entirely human, and then shoves.

When he wakes he is on an unfamiliar world, far out of reach of the Tea Shop.

After a year, he gives up on finding his way back. The Tea Shop makes sure he returns anyway.

A Moment for Self

"WHAT'S your name?"

"Beatrice."

He huffs and rolls his eyes. "Your real name."

She looks at him over her reading glasses, remnants of her last Change, quirks an eyebrow, and points a finger at where he is resting booted feet on what had been a clean table. "Off."

He rolls his eyes again and makes an exaggerated show of sitting in his chair properly.

"You get to clean that." She goes back to reading the book in her hands, red curls hiding the side of her face like a curtain.

He shrugs.

"The Shop opens in ten minutes," she says, as if the Tea Shop were conducted like a normal business. "I'd get on that if I were you." In her own way, she's warning him that a Change is coming.

Duke stands and hops over the only empty portion of the cluttered counter to grab a towel, before sauntering back around to wipe down the table he realizes is covered in the mud that had caked his boots.

"Are you keeping the red today?" Duke asks, his own drab attire looking completely out of place in the homey Tea Shop as he wipes down furniture like a busboy. Still unsure how to ask about her life and her other forms, he's gotten into a habit of inquiring about her hair color.

Business hours and hair color, we're both a couple of cowards.

She pretends not to hear this rather loud thought, and he pretends not to notice as her fingers comb wistfully through the ends of her hair. Instead he grabs a broom to do a quick sweep of the floor.

"No." She does not elaborate and closes her book without marking her place.

A clock marks the top of the hour, and the bell gives a warning trill. Duke carefully replaces the table and chair to where it had been before he had come in, then puts away the cleaning supplies. When he comes back to the front of the Tea Shop, her long red curls are gone, in their place a brown, spiked pixie cut that looks just as striking on her as the red mane. Her casual trousers and short sleeved green blouse have been replaced with a tight brown and black suit that gives her the appearance of a Doberman, complete with boots that almost match his.

She is scanning the shop with a critical eye and nearly misses the sad look that briefly passes over his face before being replaced with a wary grin.

"Good morning, Gunslinger."

She smiles at him, or tries to. The rising darkness wanting to fix his presence twists her lips into something hard and disapproving.

"I doubt my particular skill set will be utilized fully today."

Duke's pained expression gives way to an uneasy sigh. So she wasn't going into battle, which meant that, for today, the Gunslinger was needed more for her effect than her abilities.

Still, he approaches her slowly, understanding that this form would always need to be treated with caution. She lets him run his fingers down her arms until they dance in her palms, and he presses his lips against her forehead for only a moment before stepping back to look in her eyes. Her expression is unfathomable and dark, her Self giving way to the Gunslinger. It is time for him to leave.

At the door, Duke turns to face her.

"One of these days I'm going to find out your name," he gives her a wicked grin and an irreverent salute before kicking the door open.

"What makes you think I even have one?" She murmurs quietly.

Duke is fairly certain he was not meant to hear her, so he leaves without pausing. Even if she did not believe it, he knows she has a name buried deep underneath the fathomless layers of identities and titles and forms. He just hopes he is around when she finds out what it is, hopes that she will allow him to be a part of that particular adventure. And he wonders if it would be more than somebody like him would ever deserve.

The Child

"WHAT'S your name?" His voice is husky from exhaustion and residual pain. Her hands are as gentle as they can be, considering that she is stitching up the ragged and ugly looking gash that spirals down his arm with the hands of the Child. Duke is not sure if he really expects an answer or not. She has never given a straightforward answer to that question before. A fact that does not stop the surge of temper when the Child responds with only a shrug. Her smudged nose and unkempt hair do little to mask a concentration at odds with her outward appearance.

This young form of hers looks as if it should be filled with exuberance and energy, but the Child has been uncharacteristically melancholic, despite having a face meant for chasing butterflies through idyllic fields of wildflowers.

Duke grabs a mug with his free hand and takes a swig of his coffee, spiked with something that both warms and burns him. Not for the first time, he wishes she had just foregone the coffee altogether.

Another jab of the suture's needle, and he refuses to flinch at the sharp pain. He wants to look at her, wants to lose himself in watching deft hands tend near ruined flesh, but he finds himself unable to even turn his head in the Child's direction.

How many children has he left orphaned?

He doesn't usually entertain hate, yet the word does not come close to encompassing how much he detests this form of hers. What this form represents. What possible uses could it have to make sure every story on this world is kept in balance?

Innocence and violence. Hope and torment.

Like us.

How many children have her monsters destroyed?

She finishes tending to him, packs up her supplies and goes to wash her hands of his blood. She has to use a stool to reach the sink.

How many times had she been that child?

Duke knows he is barricading himself behind layers of internal walls, knows that on some level it is hurting her as well. He doesn't know how to fix it, and he damned well doesn't want to open up to a child right now.

He is halfway out the door when he hears a soft voice call his name. He slams the door behind him. A stiff drink in the darkened corner of a sleazy bar was waiting for him to drown in. She would understand. At least, he hopes she will. A part of him knows he would never forgive himself if she does not.

The Sin-Eater

HER hair is blonde today. Platinum, almost bleach white, with gold and copper highlights that fall in perfectly sculpted waves he knows hurricane force winds would not dare disturb. Duke cannot help the once-over he gives the curvy, glamourous, and nearly glowing figure she makes as she raises one thin eyebrow in amusement at his assessment. Perfectly manicured nails tap at the polished wood of the table she stands beside but does not lean against, while the other hand delicately holds a champagne flute of some sparkling golden liquid. The glittering evening gown is a shimmering match to her deadly looking heels and her hair and skin and eyelashes – the brightness of her currently sapphire eyes a shock of color in the gold.

She should look out of place amongst the rustic knick-knacks and mismatched tables of the Tea Shop, and yet even now the Shop holds her up.

Duke gives a low wolf whistle as she sashays to him and gives him a platonic peck on the cheek.

"You have horrible timing, Duke," she murmurs and takes a delicate sip from her glass.

"Who are you?" His question comes out a tad more breathy than he would ever admit to. On some level Duke already knows what the answer is, because he has never in his life been attracted to sultry blondes or flimsy elegance or sparkling wines or, dear gods, glitter, but right now his body aches to sweep her up in his arms and waltz around the Tea Shop to the tones of ethereal saxophones and sensual violins. Even as he falls deeper into her thrall, he rages against the pull of her current form.

She looks at him with the deep sadness of understanding and tries to ease the confusion of his senses by putting some distance between them.

"To you? I am a lie." The Seductress looks away from him, the sight of his anger and confused rapture pains her Self, and she feels the faintest flutter of hatred at her own form. The gut punch feeling growing in her chest is mirrored in his own realization, and his understanding destroys all traces of the captivation on his face. She lets him close the distance she has created and grab her free hand with a desperation that could have bruised a mortal.

"I'm sorry," he apologizes for something not his doing, saying the words she should be telling him. Still he searches her face until she turns her sapphire gaze to him. He is reaching for her on more than one level, and she cannot help the draw of his truths laid bare, to see them without effort for the first time. His belief hits first, the foundation of his every interaction – he does not feel worthy. Of anything.

The champagne glass trembles in her hands as she sets it down, and then there is another under her skin. An old one, full of pain, and desperate to ease the guilt of others. Her Self steps aside without hesitation, letting the elder form reach for Duke, cupping his face in gentle hands.

Her eyes have turned black, her blonde hair crackles in silent electricity, and her skin splits like fractured porcelain. The Tea Shop is gone, replaced with a web of dead roots and barren soil and stone grey skies. He reels back but her grip is firm and unforgiving.

"Let me," the Sin-Eater comforts.

"No," Duke scrabbles at her hands as he feels something dark and staining pulled from him, the weight of his own personal ledger easing under her careful administrations. He finally wrenches from her. Too late, for already he feels lighter, cleaner at levels he did not know he had.

They are back to where they started. The Seductress and the fixer stare at each other from opposite ends of a picturesque Tea Shop whose walls have seen almost as many stories form and evolve as there have been stories written down.

"Those weren't your burdens to carry!" He is furious, and while some of her forms do not understand why, the rest are satisfied with the result. They have never before given a gift unprompted or unrequired, as they were not meant to choose whom they gifted. So Duke's strange response is ignored by all except the Self. She buries herself under the others, unsure how else to respond, and knowing that she is taking the easy way out.

The Self is gone, leaving only the Seductress behind. He growls loudly in the silence and internally rages against her uncaring serenity.

"I'm late for an appointment, Duke." As usual she is waiting for him to leave first.

He angrily kicks over a chair and storms out of the Tea Shop. He does not look back and it is almost a year before he returns again.

A Prophecy

SHE stands on the roof of the Tea Shop and watches as *The Curious Lass* parts the city as easily as if it were the sea, the denizens of this world shifting their own courses to accommodate the Great Ship without noticing why. The sudden rift sends glimmering ripples through the city, every dust mite floating in the air and grain of sand trembling on the streets glittering with the lights of shifting time.

An anxiety within most of her selves eases at the sight of the striking figure standing at the bow of the ship, a wind of the ship's own making causing red hair and sails to whip dramatically in the changing light. She raises a hand in greeting, then holds it out to help the other step onto the roof with her.

"Captain." She says in lieu of a greeting.

It is the Lass who looks at her through Captain Valentine's features, eyes swirling silver and black in a galactic dance. The tightness in her chest that had eased at the presence of her ally, returns in force at the reminder of the being behind the other woman's keen gaze.

When the Lass speaks, the air around them stills. She feels the power of the other drawing at her forms.

"Seer."

The Seer strengthens under her skin, imbuing her form with its presence, and a sudden understanding of the distant storm presses against her senses. She blinks.

The Twins would fail one last time in their attempts to force a balance on the world, and the Nameless One would hold destruction in its hand. A child of infinite potential, born of both Otherland and another land, would be given a choice the Nameless One was never allowed to have. All would end in fire, and from fire something new would be born.

The Seer opens her eyes and Valentine is squeezing her hand in comfort. Her eyes are still those of the Lass, but her gaze is that of the pirate captain. They watch the sunset in companionable silence, then watch the nightlife of the city below, until it too is quiet and still.

She shakes off the duties of the Seer, the newest Self pressing at some invisible boundary keeping her locked away.

"Would you really curse another child with this?" she gestures at herself, as dark cracks begin to split the skin on her arm.

Valentine squeezes her hand again and turns to face her. Even in the darkest hour of the night the stars and moonlight filter through the sails of the Great Ship, making her eyes and hair gleam.

"I know the wound that festers here," it is only Valentine speaking, and she places her hand over the Self's chest.

"You were given a choice."

"Yes," Valentine's expression twists with the echoes of a long-ago pain. "And you were not. That is never meant to happen."

The Self does not reply as the pirate captain gathers her words. The Lass reaches out and brushes a thumb across the split skin on the back of the Self's hand, easing the pain and lending her own brand of support to them both.

"When the Twins took a child of infinite potential and destroyed it to create you, they corrupted something deep within this land that cannot be healed by either of us. Your purpose has been to inspire legends, incite heroes – you are a manufactured catalyst forcing stories onto those 'deemed' to have 'potential.'" Valentine spits out the last words with a fury the other had never witnessed.

No one is born without potential.

The thought comes from them both.

"And if this other child refuses?" She has to know, is desperate to know in a way completely unattached to her forms or purpose.

"Then nothing will be reborn from the wreckage of the coming storm," the Lass says solemnly. The air moves quietly around them, the night sky a shimmering, cold blanket above their heads.

"If the child meets me, it will destroy what little chance this world has," the Harbinger manages to break through the other forms, reminding them that her very existence is a threat to providing the child an honest choice.

"I know," the voice is that of both Valentine and the Lass.

"There are few in Otherland who could spend a lifetime without crossing paths with the Tea Shop."

"I know."

What would you have me do?

"Let your own story unfold," there is no command in the Lass' tone, nor does she expand on her meaning, though the beginnings of an amused grin are rather telling.

"Duke?" she blurts out his name in surprise.

"You two are connected in a way that even I do not fully comprehend," the Lass nods. "But I can see enough to know that wherever that connection came from, it must be protected." The Lass looks away, and something in her bearing shifts uncomfortably.

"What did you do to him?"

"Nothing that cannot be undone, should the need arise."

"What did you do?"

"I bound him to your life source – do not rage at me, Beast," the command is quick and brutally effective against the other form that struggles to break free. The Self's chest squeezes with a sharp pain.

"How could you?"

"I did what I had to do to save his life." The Lass is unrepentant, though her tone is tinged with Valentine's sadness.

"Does he know?"

"Not yet. He suspects, I think, but is, for now, happy to remain unaware."

"He will find out," her voice is that of the Harbinger once more. The darkness of the night shifts around them, and one of her forms can feel the first sign of sunlight over the edge of the horizon.

"Yes," the Lass replies. "And when the time comes, you will be more prepared to help him understand what it means. For you both."

They do not speak as the night gives way to dawn, and it is Valentine that pulls her in for an embrace.

"I can't promise to be by your side at the end," the pirate captain's voice is full of honest regret. "But you will not be alone when you face the storm." The words are a promise she holds close as the Great Ship gently dives back through rippling streets of the city below.

A Moment of Self

"DO you live time in order?"

She stills, briefly, but does not answer. She is not sure she has a good answer to the question, at least not from his perspective.

He notices her hesitance and tries another tactic.

"How many times have we met?"

"One hundred and twenty-seven." She watches him from the corner of her eyes, hoping she has correctly accounted for the visits they both have yet to make. He mentally counts their interactions in confusion. "You would not remember your twenty-third time. You were unconscious."

"I... wait, what?"

"You tangled with a dragon, who was kind enough to return you after teaching you a lesson in humility."

Duke's eyes widen in comical disbelief and a growing realization. "You were the one who fixed me up after that?"

She smiles and gives a slight nod as she places a little bonsai tree in the light of one of the windows. Duke narrows his eyes.

"Wait a minute. What do you mean return me?" She disappears behind the counter and begins making him his customary beverage. He tries not to let the smell distract him. "Well?"

The mug was steaming and large in her latest form's small hands. Her eyes gleam with humor as she sets it front of him, one hand trailing teasingly to his shoulder.

"I may have let it slip to a few of the greater beings of this world that if you were found in any compromising situations you should be returned here for... safe keeping."

He had almost let the coffee distract him. He fights not to spit his drink up his nose.

"You said what!?" He does not know whether to laugh or rage at her, though the absurdity of the situation eventually wins out. She is clearly enjoying his incredulous attitude, giggling behind her hand like a girl caught on the more amusing side of a prank.

"I probably used somewhat different words," she says airily and saunters back to other side of counter, this time returning with another, less identifiable plant. "But I think that was the general drift of it." She nods, as if confirming her words to herself.

She is teasing him.

He laughs, full bellied and loud until tears form at the corners of his eyes.

"Great," he snorts. "Now all of Otherland thinks I'm your wayward pet."

"Perhaps," her grin is mischievous, and does not fully fit the face of her current form. He rolls his eyes and chuckles.

He finishes his mug and hops over the counter to wash it. Out of the corner of his eye he watches her. She is a picture of relaxation and is – or at least seems to be – newly preoccupied with the strange flower-bush-vine-thing on the table in front of her.

"Well, I guess that's alright then," he finally says, smiling at her. She does not look up from her task, but the smile she gives in return is definitely all hers.

Charlie the Dog

"I got a dog," he tells her in lieu of a greeting. He is covered in dust and grime, thirsty from a job on a world without water, and is still wearing a rough desert tunic and head scarf.

"Oh?" She is drawing something on a large piece of discolored parchment and does not look up from her work, but her attention has shifted to him.

"Yeah, her name is Charlie."

She snorts indelicately and the glimmer of humor in her eyes when she shoots him a glance tells of a story he has not yet had a chance to hear. She finishes some intricate detail on what he is beginning to recognize as a chart and finally looks up at him.

"For goodness' sake, Duke, sit down," she huffs. "You look like you're about to keel over."

"I thought you didn't like it when I got the furniture dirty," Duke responds with all the maturity of a two-year-old sticking his tongue out in defiance, and receives a gentle cuff in response. "Hey!" He rubs the back of his head indignantly, though he sits anyway.

The glass of water set in front of him is something of a welcome surprise, as is the fondly teasing "Baby" that accompanies it. She goes back behind the counter once more, and he downs the water in one go, surprised to find his thirst finally eased.

When she returns, it is with his more customary dark coffee drink and a steaming cup of her own.

"Charlie likes people food," he grins. "Actually, Charlie just likes pizza, mashed potatoes, and pumpkin pie." He shrugs at her expression. "Don't look at me in that tone of voice. I don't know why my dog has such weird tastes."

She smirks over her mug. "Perhaps she takes after her human."

Duke's snarky smile cracks into a laugh. He takes a drink from the hot mug of coffee.

"Perhaps she does."

It is not until later that week, when he has finally stumbled back to his own place and Charlie is nosing through a bag of treats that had been slipped into his hand as he left the Tea Shop, that Duke realizes he had not seen anyone else behind her gaze his entire visit. Charlie woofs softly at his sudden stillness and he does not hide the sudden tightness behind his eyes.

"You'll meet her someday, girl." He scratches the retriever's ears and gives her a gentle head bump. "One of these days."

The Jester

"SO," Duke grins and hops up to sit cross-legged on one of the tables of the Tea Shop. "Guess what." He looks for all the worlds like a mischievous boy about to run off and do something foolish and exhilarating. She quirks an eyebrow at him but does not speak. Her silence makes him all the more determined to coax words from her. He could be an excited canine wagging its whole body for all the energy that he is exuding.

She decides to humor him.

With the smooth grace of an acrobat she leaps up onto the small table then sits across from him, mirroring his pose. The Jester laughs at the gobsmacked look on his face.

"You look like a fish, Duke," she pokes him in the chest and he closes his mouth with a snap, narrowing his eyes before tugging on one of her braids.

"For that I'm not telling." He crosses his arms and sticks his nose in the air.

"Not telling what to whom?" She looks sideways at him.

"Not telling you that...." He glares at her. "Oh, you're sneaky."

She shrugs. "It almost worked."

"Almost only counts in horseshoes," he pauses, suddenly distracted. "You know, that's one saying I can honestly say I don't understand. Though it probably has something to do with the game."

He trails off in thought and she bumps her knees against his. "You were going to tell me something?"

"Nope, you didn't guess."

"If I guess, will it stop you from," she waves her arms at him ambiguously, "this?"

He attempts to look thoughtful, though his fingers drumming an excited beat against his leg give him away. "Maybe?"

"Then I'm not guessing," she says, and bursts out laughing at the dawning realization and subsequent grin that returns to Duke's face.

"Then I'll continue to be adorably annoying." Duke practically wiggles.

She leans forward suddenly, her hands pressing against his shoulders, though not pushing. "Then I will guess that you have something fun to tell me," she whispers in his ear, and the Jester launches herself into a handstand using his shoulders as a platform. "And I will use you to practice for my show later today."

Duke's response is instinctive, arms coming up to help steady her, despite the more than apparent lack of need, his body moving in subtle counterbalance. She raises one hand and grabs a foot that has fallen gently in front of her face.

"Are you going to make me stay like this all afternoon?" she asks, and brings her other leg down to tap his hair with her foot. "Or are you going to tell me the news?" Duke wants to poke at her feet like an antagonistic child, but is much more loath to disrupt her.

"Charlie had puppies!" He grins up at her and sees the honest warmth in her gaze before the Jester takes over, laughing as she vaults off his shoulders to land en pointe on one of the chairs. From the chair, she leaps, spins, and swings around the Tea Shop in the parody of a waltz.

For a moment he does not see the pigtail braids and black eyes, or skintight, brightly colored jester suit, or the hint of doll makeup that covers every inch of exposed flesh. Light radiates from her, warming every corner of the space. She finally stills, out of breath with laughter.

"Can I meet them?" she asks, wondering if the back door would allow her to leave for such a mundane errand.

"Sweetheart," Duke drawls. "You can have first pick of the litter."

The Warrior

SHE feels him giving in to death seconds before the back door swings open, and the bell above the front door announces that the Lass has arrived.

"Go to him," the Lass gives her the permission she would not have asked for.

As soon as she crosses the threshold, she knows this is the moment the Lass had spoken of on the rooftop. Her choice now was going to change him. She does not spare the back door a glance before moving into the darkened wasteland of another world.

It seems he was always meant to die like this, scrabbling and choking and struggling for a survival he was not sure he even wanted. Raging against the dying of the light and all that poetic nonsense. The majority of his life had barely been a life at all. He could finally see how it resembled his pending death in too many ways.

He should have gotten a pet. A hamster or a squirrel or a dog or something. If by some curse he survived, he was going to find himself a companion. And find the Tea Shop. He should never have stopped searching for a way back.

The coughing gets worse. Duke can taste the blood at the back of his throat and gags against it. He considers wiping his mouth, then wonders if it would actually help. His whole body is an open wound, filthy and desiccating even as he still breathes.

How long has it been? The cold in the air changes. When the first dirty, stained, polluted snow begins to fall, he stops struggling. Duke gives in, unable to keep pulling himself through the muck in search of a destination, in search of the one person he cannot name.

She finds him anyway.

Duke is staring at the snow and mud near his face when he feels the air shift. The blood that has been pooling in patterns around him warps as if drawn to a force stronger even than that of the earth below it. He lets his senses appreciate the graphic beauty of his own blood being pulled from the snowy ground by something unseen.

"You shouldn't be here," he coughs out, barely audible, rust-like flecks staining his cracked lips.

"Neither should you," a shadowed voice echoes around him, backlit with the brilliance of righteous anger.

He wants to tell her more. To warn her. Her presence has already begun drawing the monsters from their resting places. The light and life that shone from underneath her skin a beacon to the creatures of this world. They feed off it – exactly why his enemies had dumped him here.

The Warrior kneels at his side and gently places a gloved hand to his cheek. He blinks, and has to pry his eyes back open to keep them from getting stuck closed. Her armor and eyes are flashing, a gleaming reflection of a light not produced in this world. The warmth of her hand, covered as it was, eases the last of the rage he held toward the coming darkness.

Sucking, skittering noises erupt into a dull roar around them, and the Warrior stands, sword drawn. She plants herself over him like the bringer of death, and her sword flashes in an elegant dance.

He thinks maybe the battle rages on for days.

The Warrior could have ended it in that first moment, but she draws it out, lets the carnage pile up around them as she strikes down all those that had leeched at his life. She never falters. Never wavers. When at last she relents, her shining sword bloody and dripping, she lets her voice carry through what is left of the agonized land.

Later, when the blood is washed away and the open wounds are stitched, he wonders if it was all a dream. If he imagined her words, and the blazing light that had surrounded them, in the haze of disbelief that he was being rescued. After a few months of silent, wordless visits to the Tea Shop, he decides that it does not matter if it was a dream. He can feel her truths in a way that he never has before, and that was real enough for him. It was time to for him to go find himself a puppy.

He. Is. Mine.

Aftermath of the Beast

THE Tea Shop is in shambles. Scorch marks are scattered along the walls and floor, chairs are upended, and tables lay in piles of broken kindling. Pained whimpering echoes around the Shop, interrupted only by harsh, raspy breathing. The puppy Duke has been taking with him to train growls, tailed curled tight under its belly as the small body shifts in agitation. Duke reaches down and gives her a comforting scratch behind the ears.

"Easy, girl," he murmurs. "Where are they, little one?"

He falls deep into his old habits, a lifetime of calculated manipulation and violence rushing to the surface, focused wholly on the potential threat to his safe haven.

The puppy quiets at the instinctive hand movement he usually uses to put Charlie on alert, and a part of his brain is pleased that the puppy is picking up on more than he had noticed.

He follows the pained sounds to the furthest, darkest corner of the Tea Shop. He registers breathing from both the woman and the small furry body in her lap, but he can see their shaking, and smell the sharp tang of blood.

"Stay, girl." Duke orders the small retriever at his side, and approaches them cautiously.

She is staring into the depths of something, eyes glassy and vacant. Her hands alternate between clutching and stroking the injured puppy in her lap. Blood covers her hands where she has pressed them against the puppy's wound, a wound that from what he can see has long since stopped bleeding. The puppy shivers in the woman's grasp, every once in a while twisting in an attempt to lick her hands or nuzzle against her – though whether for its own comfort or hers Duke is not sure.

He kneels, and cups her face in his hands, stroking a rough thumb over her cheeks.

"Hey," his voice more a request than a greeting. "I need you to look at me, yeah?" She turns her face towards to the sound of his voice but does not acknowledge him. He begins cataloging everything about her appearance, the untorn clothes, the lack of injuries, the network of faint lines that covered her skin.

"Come on, now, sweetheart," his grip on her face tightens slightly. "Come back to us. You're worrying the children." The puppies both whimper as if on cue, but his attempt at levity falls flat even to his own ears. He cannot tell if it is his ill executed joking or the cold puppy nose shoving against her hand that was bringing awareness slowly back to her, and honestly he doesn't care what does the trick as long as it works.

She takes a deep, unsteady breath, her wounded gaze dropping from his to the puppy. The shaking starts in her hands and spreads from there.

"Hey now," he tries to offer comfort and pushes back the urge to track down whatever has done this and skin it alive. "It's gone for the moment."

She let out a raw, scraping laugh that makes him and the puppies cringe. He presses his forehead to hers.

"Who did this to you?"

A tear finally slides silently down her cheek, and when she answers, her voice sounds small and distant.

"I did."

"What?" He pulls back to get a good look at her then lets his gaze wander across the chaos of the Tea Shop.

"The Beast." She trembles even as she begins to collect herself.

Realization is far too slow in coming. One of her own forms had brought this destruction, the heart of the Tea Shop – the bell and the back door – the only things protected from its wrath. He looks at the puppy in her arms and realizes what she must have faced when the Beast was finally pulled back. His heart aches for them both.

"What they created is monstrous," she whispers to him.

"Hey, no," he forces her to look him in the eye. "No. What they did to you is monstrous, but that doesn't make you one." Not for the first time, Duke wishes he could go back and destroy her makers before they ever had the chance of getting their hands on her. Even if it meant he would have died or lost himself ages ago. Even if it meant the same for her.

"You have to take him back," she cracks a bit around the edges, tears still falling quietly from her wide eyes. Both of the puppies let out a whine. Duke shakes his head. She growls at him.

"Nothing living is safe with me for long," her voice has a practical edge to it, and Duke is pretty sure it is the voice of the Advocate, an attempt to make herself feel more rational. He slides down to sit beside her, pulling her against him as they lean against the wall of the Tea Shop, partially destroyed by the creature of rage that lived within her.

"That puppy chose you," he says into her hair. "I don't think you could get rid of him if you tried." He gives a sad smile when the puppy licks at his hand, and the other abandons her post at the door to come and curl up next to her littermate.

They sit like that, the four of them, for well over an hour. Each drifting in and out of sleep, none willing to move from the safety of each other's presence. Duke holds them close, desperately begging the Tea Shop to keep them safe, promising in return to never let her face the aftermath of the Beast alone.

Before the Storm

"I sent the dog to your cabin."

"Why?"

She does not answer, and he feels the first thread of alarm, a tightness in his throat that began when she called her overgrown puppy just a dog. Something with her, or between them, was shifting in a direction he was not going to like.

"How many times have we met?" She changes the subject, and begins to pace, her skin nearly vibrating with energy. The Harbinger was stirring beneath the surface in anticipation, waiting for her moment to be the unleasher of heroes and stories.

"Why do you ask?" He schools his features and voice to sound as casual as he can, though he knows she can see through it if she wishes to. She sits in the chair across from him and grabs his hand. The tightness spreads to his chest.

"Something is..." A struggle plays out behind her eyes, a battle of wills between herself and the role she is meant to play. He lets his thumb rub across her palm. "Something is coming, and it could change things." As much as he wants to, Duke does not press, letting her find her own words.

"It could – it will – irrevocably change things in this world," she finally continues. "Doors and time windows and destinies all jumbled up. These things could keep you from coming back, or switch up my timeline, and..." She trails off again and this time Duke feels a sudden sense of desperation at what is not being said.

"What aren't you telling me?" he asks quietly.

"I don't know if I am meant to live through this," she finally admits, and looks at him in that bland way she sometimes got when she knew what she was about to say would upset him. Suddenly, something within her settles, as if by finally saying it aloud, the internal struggle from before is gone. It infuriates him more than he could, or would, ever want to explain.

"And what?!" He kicks himself back from the table, tea cups and coffee spilling to the floor. "This is just... it? You're okay with this?"

She shrugs, any trace of earlier nervousness gone. If he had not just been watching her pace around the Tea House like a caged wolf, he would never have known, or believed, that she feels anything other than apathy to her latest "destiny."

"How many times have we met, Duke?" she asks again. "For all the years we've known each other, can you count how many times we have met? Did you really think it was going to last forever?"

"That's not fair, and you know it!"

For a while she does not respond, and he is tempted to force the conversation forward. She remains in her seat, staring almost defiantly at him.

"Two hundred and seventy-six times in half a dozen years or so, *for you*" she says it slowly, as if trying to find a way to explain what came next to a child. "Do you want to know how many more times you will come to visit? Do you have any idea how old I actually am?"

Her questions stop him cold. It was never something he had really thought about. Or wanted to. She stands and in one fluid motion has grabbed his face in her hands, eyes intense and hard in the soft light of the Tea Shop.

"I have lived," she struggles in finding the right words. "I have existed for so many lifetimes, more than even I can count. The stories – the lives I have influenced and changed..." She presses her forehead against his, and lets the emotions of her truth crack through her calm. "Duke, you should not even exist."

He tries to protest. She squeezes her hands and shakes her head.

"Duke," she whispers. "Duke, there are demons inside this form that know only rage, and darkness, and revenge. Creatures, beasts, that are meant only to incite heroes to vengeance." Her voice fades to a murmur, but he can still hear every word. *"Fury and blood, a depth of madness to rival the stars, and nothing, nothing that can keep the raging dark at bay for long.* Life is not safe in my presence; it is how I was made. Why I was made."

Duke reaches up and grasps her face in his hands, a gentler mirror to her own position. The denial he holds is an aching, physical pain. "What are you saying?"

"I'm not real, Duke." She does not know how to convince him to let her go. To be okay with her leaving. She does not want him to wait for her, to wait on someone who will likely never arrive. "I am a tool, the creation and product of self-serving gods in a vain attempt to maintain the balance of this world. If that balance is restored, my purpose fades. If saving this world requires my life, then that is what I must give."

"Don't be a martyr," he growls.

"You might be surprised at how often the Martyr has made an appearance," she says wryly, finally opening her eyes to peer into his. Her gaze begs him to understand.

"You have been the only decent thing in my sorry excuse for an existence," he confesses. "You can't abandon me now."

"It is not up to us." She pulls away from him and kneels to begin picking up the pieces of the shattered teacup.

He stands, looking over the Tea Shop, eyes and chest tight in an emotion he is entirely unused to.

"I don't know if I can accept that," he admits, knowing on some level that he is coming dangerously close to ending something between them prematurely, despite the fact that she is trying to push him away.

She does not stand or look at him, carefully, deliberately, picking up each piece of broken china.

"Then I suggest you avoid the Tea Shop until the coming storm passes," she finally answers.

The slam of the door echoes around the Tea Shop, the silence that follows is cold, and final.

Rabbit

SHE sits on the edge of the roof and stares at the quiet town square, still muted by the morning fog. Pre-dawn light gives the movement of the early birds a ghostlike quality, and even from her vantage point obscures the details of the building across from her. She closes her eyes against the growing light.

Awaking to the knowledge of a coming Change is irksome, though she tries to pretend that she does not know why. Today she would become someone else, at least in part, and she would not know who until the Tea Shop below opened. So she breathes in the early morning, pressing her fingers into the shingles, and listens.

A man below is drinking coffee, brewed with chicory, hot cream, but just a little, his steps regular until he takes a sip. The snake that lives in the alley behind to the Tea Shop is contemplating moving one alleyway over, closer to the vent connected to another shop's kitchen. She takes another breath and takes in the scent of dew and fog fading into light. The sun's rays hit the back of her eyelids and the bell over the front door chimes a tune only she can hear.

She knows that when she opens her eyes, she will be back in the Tea Shop, topped with the trappings of another form, her Self buried too deep to recall.

Except when the bell finally stops its private chiming, and the sun's rays finish pushing through the remnants of the mist, she is still on a rooftop. Only now she is sitting above a different, somewhat busier town square with less familiar store fronts. The air is pungent in an unpleasant, rancid, food-and-human sort of way, yet muted as if it has wafted in from some far-off city to what appears to be a small township area. She can hear metal horseshoes smacking on cobblestones and the rustle of an unshod child sneaking through still-wet grass.

She looks at her hands and realizes that the only thing that has changed about her are her clothes. From the time she has begun, this has never happened, except with Duke. She always got to stay the same for Duke.

The barefoot child draws nearer. She finds herself sitting on the ground, surrounded by shrubs and grasses and a few autumn trees on the bank of a slow-moving river.

"Rabbit! Come back, little Rabbit," the child calls in mock whisper. "Where did he go?" the child asks herself.

The Self listens, intrigued, and is surprised to find that not only was there no rabbit, no rabbit had passed this way in a while. Curious.

"Gotcha!" The child pushes through the shrubbery and pounces on her foot, both hands grabbing around her ankle. "Rabbit?" The girl, face predictably smudged with dirt, peers up at her quizzically.

She peers back in amusement. "Rabbit?" she asks.

The child lets go of her foot and stands, arms crossed, and pouts at her.

"That's not fair, you changed," the child states, matter of fact.

"What's your name?"

The girl rolls her eyes. "It's Alice," she huffs. "And you're supposed to be a rabbit."

"Am I?"

"Yes. What's it like?" Alice asks, though she seems distracted and not at all paying attention despite the query.

"What is what like?" she responds.

"What's it like being a rabbit?" Alice says as if the question should have been obvious.

"Do I look like a rabbit?"

"No, but you must be one."

"Why do you say that?"

"My rabbit was there, and then gone, and then you were there," Alice stops as if that explained everything. The Self smiles.

"And that makes me a rabbit?"

"It makes you *my* rabbit."

She stretches her toes into the grass and looks up at the sky. "Well then, little Alice, what is it you would like to do with your rabbit?"

Alice tugs at a few blades of grass and follows the other's gaze into the clouds. The silence stretches out between them until the Self and the quickly emerging Rabbit wonder if the child does not know herself what she wants. Alice reaches out and grabs her hand.

"Let's go on an adventure."

Thank you, dear readers, for taking the time to dip your toes into the world of Otherland with me. If you enjoyed Nameless, and want to know what happens next, please keep your eye out for the forthcoming, full-length novel:

Pirates of Otherland

They say there is a ship that can sail anywhere. Land, sea, and sky are but clear waters to her shining keel and sunlight sparkles on the very sands of time as she passes. Her captain is brilliant in mind, striking in dress, and as quick in a duel of wits as she is in one of swords. Together, the captain, the ship, and her crew sail for otherworldly treasure on the waves of adventure, every one buccaneers to the last. And the ship, well, The Curious Lass takes care of her own, on her own terms. No vessel, be it mortal or Otherland, has courted such a reputation for prank and mad humour as she... and it will take all her wit and cunning to face the coming storm.

Fifty years have passed since Alice was forced to abandon Otherland, leaving behind her husband and a life of enchantment and adventure. But a mysterious letter, a friendly fox, and a painting composed in a trance are about to change everything. Now, not only will Alice have to face the world and people she once called home, her grandchildren are about to discover the secrets she has been keeping all these years...

ABOUT THE AUTHOR

Dawn M. Keiser is a dancer, traveler, and artist with a penchant for strong coffee, unplanned road trip adventures, and enthusiastically jumping into new interests. She balances work with dreaming up tales of talking animals and sentient pirate ships, practicing as a casual aerialist, and hanging out with her dogs and cat. Somehow in all this, Dawn also manages to continue her studies in space operations, human factors, and systems engineering.

www.dawnmkeiser.com
www.undertheredfedora.com